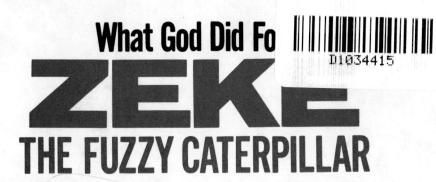

What God Did Fo

ZEKE
THE FUZZY CATERPILLAR

by Robert O'Rourke   illustrated by John Ham

These were long days for Zeke . . .
  Slow, easy days to think.
Curled up in his snug cocoon
  with the sunshine warming him,

He could remember another time
                   another place
                   another life
When he was a caterpillar.

Oh, but he was busy then . . .
  Dodging big trucks on the road
  Climbing up fence posts
  Crawling across fields
    but
    mostly

he was busy eating everything . . .
    leaves
    grass
    flowers
    anything green and growing!
It had been a time for taking!

All around him there was giving!
His favorite tree soaked up sunshine,
   but it gave back juicy, red apples.
The old river took in tiny streams,
   but it gave water to the clouds
   so there would be rain.

Even the bird who pecked a hundred seeds
gave back pretty songs!
What could he give?

Curled up in his cocoon,
  Zeke could only remember taking . . .
    sunshine
    dewdrops
    green things.

He knew he could never give
back anything like . . .
juicy red apples
or raindrops
or happy songs.

But long ago
  in the very beginning of things
God had a wonderful plan
  for you and me

trees
rivers
birds
And even little, fuzzy caterpillars
like Zeke!

God gave us all
  the gift of life.
And
The secret and purpose of life
  is to return to God
  a very special gift . . .

a beautiful life!
Because . . .
   Everyone can give that gift.

As the sun warmed his snug cocoon,
Zeke slowly began to waken.
It was as if each sunray gave him
    new energy—new life.

He twisted and turned
He strained and pushed . . .
   And suddenly his cocoon broke open.

Zeke squeezed through the hole
 onto a very high limb.
He felt himself all over . . .
 Where were his short, stubby legs?
 Where had his soft, fuzzy hair gone?

His long, wiggly body was gone, too.
Instead he felt wings . . .
  And graceful long legs
  And big brown eyes.

As Zeke warmed in the sun,
He felt little zingy, alive feelings inside.
He wanted to . . .
    sail on a breeze
    follow a sunbeam
    kiss a flower

And suddenly it happened . . .
He was part of the world again.

This time he floated over the fields
instead of bumping along the ground.

Zeke loved what he had become.

Now it was a time for giving!
This time, he thought,
I'll give something special back . . .

not apples
or rain clouds
or songs.

This time I will give . . .
  bright colors
  grace
  beauty!
Zeke felt wonderful!